Snow Day!
A Winter Tale

By Joan Holub
Illustrated by Will Terry

SCHOLASTIC INC.
New York Toronto London Auckland
Sydney Mexico City New Delhi Hong Kong

For Kristen Shaheen,
an award-winning ice skater
–J. H.

ISBN: 978-0-545-22597-7

12 11 10 9 8 7 6   11 12 13 14/0

Printed in the U.S.A.   40

First Scholastic printing, December 2009

Designed by Lisa Vega
The text of this book was set in font Century Oldstyle BT.

"Snowflake,"
said Jake.

"Snowball," said Paul.

"Snow ant," said Grant.

"Snow sled," said Ed.

"Hop on," said Dawn.

"Me too," said Sue.
"Me three," said Dee.

"Ready. Set," said Brett.

"Push! Go!" said Joe.

Whoosh!

"Quick! Quick!"
said Nick.

"Slow! Slow!"
said Joe.

"Wheee!"
said Dee.

"Nooo!" said Joe.

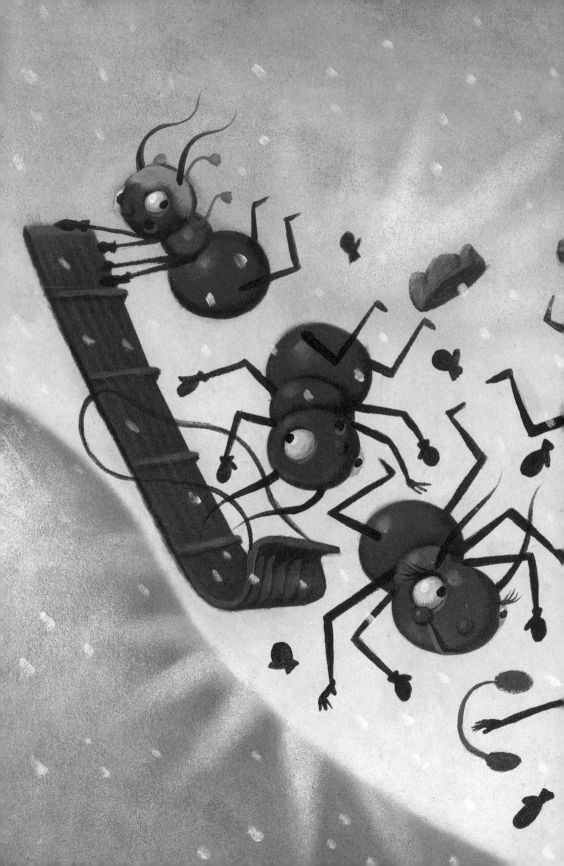

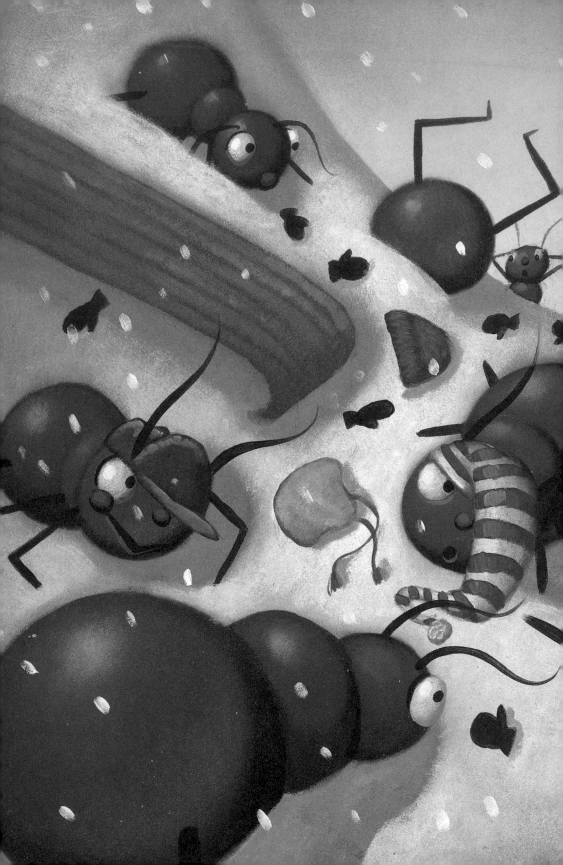

"Again?" asked Jen.

"Yes! Go!" said Joe.